ROOSEVELT
AND THE MAGIC BOX

R. ROGERS, F. SPARACINO, & S. VANVOORHIS
ILLUSTRATED BY MICHAEL MIRACLE

BOOK
BUDDY™

With special thanks to Richard R. Rogers,
Angela and Gaspare Sparacino, Gerald Miracle,
Neureul Miracle, Lisa Stokely, Ken Post,
and all those who made this book a reality.

Text Copyright © 1994 by Book Buddy Publishing Co., Inc.
Illustrations Copyright © 1994 by Michael Miracle

Library of Congress Catalog Card Number: 94–96311

ISBN 0–9642564–9–5

Printed in the United States of America

3 5 7 9 10 8 6 4 2
PC

ROOSEVELT
AND THE MAGIC BOX

Roosevelt was playing in the park when he saw some older boys playing baseball. He walked over and asked if he could play with them.

"Go home, baby. You're too small to play in this game," they said.

Roosevelt was a small boy, because he was only eight years old. He couldn't even reach his mother's cookie jar yet.

Needless to say his feelings were hurt, and he ran home crying to his mother.

Roosevelt found his mother in the kitchen at home. She could see that he had been crying. He told her about the boys in the park.

"They said I'm too small," Roosevelt cried.

His mother held him close. "I know the older boys can be very mean sometimes, but what they don't remember is that at one time they were little too," she said.

Roosevelt felt a little bit better.

"Why don't you play in the magic box daddy helped you make, and when dinner is ready I'll call you," his mother said as she gave him a kiss on the cheek.

Roosevelt kept his magic box in his bedroom. He had drawn pictures all over the box. There were clouds on the top, and trees on the sides. Inside was a place where he could read his favorite books and imagine that he was a dinosaur tracker.

He crawled inside feeling kind of lonely. A pile of books lay in a corner of the box. He curled up with his favorite dinosaur book to read, thinking about dinosaur tracking, but soon fell asleep.

Then something amazing happened...

Kaboom! Kaboom! Kaboom!

"What was that?" Roosevelt woke up with a start.

He peeked his head out of the box and found that he was no longer in his room. Instead, he found himself in a dark forest. Tall trees were all around. The soft carpet of his bedroom was replaced with dirt and rocks. He heard the sounds of strange animals from far away.

"Where am I?" Roosevelt wondered. At first he was afraid, but he said to himself, "I am a dinosaur tracker, and dinosaur trackers are never afraid." This made him feel braver.

Roosevelt looked down at his feet and saw what could only be dinosaur tracks. He was starting to realize where he was. He followed the tracks, and they led deep into the forest. Soon he came upon a small dinosaur sitting on a rock. Roosevelt could not believe his eyes.

Roosevelt walked a little closer to get a better look. He was scared at first, but he soon saw that the dinosaur had been crying. He felt sorry for the dinosaur and wondered what was wrong.

Just then, the dinosaur looked up and saw Roosevelt standing there.

"What's the matter?" Roosevelt asked.

"The other dinosaurs made fun of me because I couldn't reach the high branches in the trees, so I ran away. Now I'm lost and I can't find my mom," said the dinosaur.

Roosevelt looked up at the trees. "Well, I can't reach the branches either. I can't even reach the cookie jar at home yet. Don't be afraid. I'll help you find your mom. My name is Roosevelt, what's yours?"

"Amy," she said. "I'm an Apatosaurus."

"I'm pleased to meet you," said Roosevelt. "I'm a dinosaur tracker, and dinosaur trackers are never afraid."

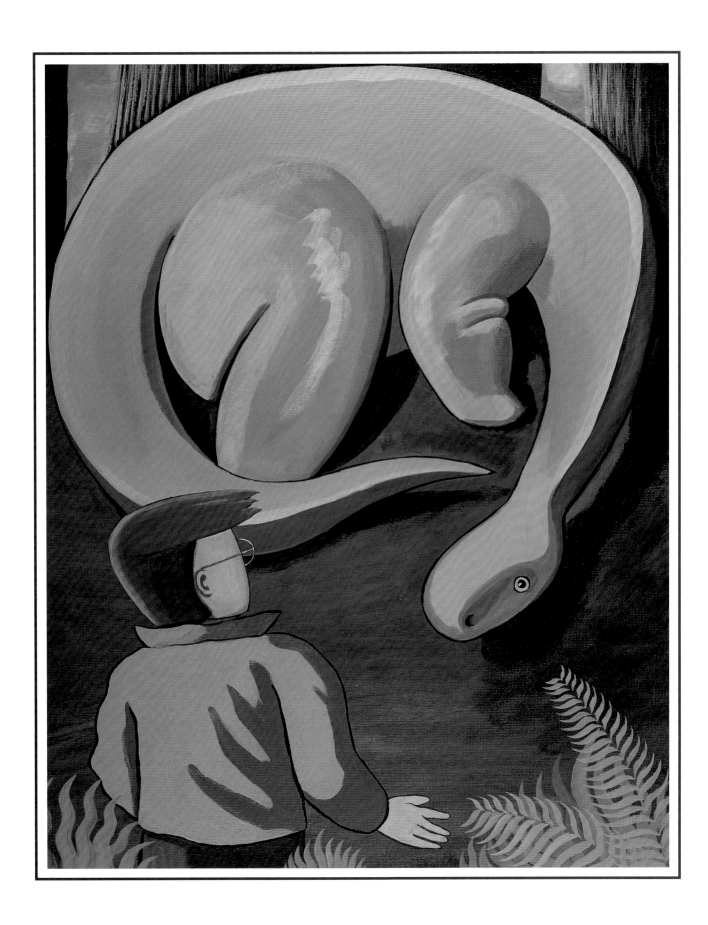

Amy and Roosevelt set out to search for Amy's mom. They followed some tracks until they came to a large tree that had fallen across their path.

Amy said that she couldn't climb over it, but thought that she could lift Roosevelt up for a look on the other side. She picked him up with her strong tail. In a moment Roosevelt was standing on the top side of the tree.

"If you were any bigger, I don't think I could have lifted you," Amy said.

Roosevelt thought about that, and for the first time he didn't mind being small. Then he saw a big dinosaur through the trees, and it turned out to be Amy's mom.

Amy's mother looked just like Amy, only she was much bigger. Roosevelt had to stretch his neck just to look up at her.

"Hello. My name is Roosevelt!" he introduced himself.

"My name is Mrs. Apatosaurus," said Amy's mom. "It's nice to meet you."

Amy told her mother how Roosevelt had helped her. Mrs. Apatosaurus had been looking for Amy and was very grateful to Roosevelt. She told them that they were both very brave.

Roosevelt told her about how he had come to their forest in his magic box, and followed the dinosaur tracks he had found. Mrs. Apatosaurus thought Roosevelt was a brave dinosaur tracker.

"I think Roosevelt should be getting home now, because it is getting late and his mother will be looking for him," Mrs. Apatosaurus said. "Why don't both of you climb on my back and we will go find Roosevelt's magic box."

They went back through the forest and found Roosevelt's magic box right where he had left it. As Roosevelt climbed inside, he waved goodbye to his new friends. He said to himself, "I wish I could see my mom again."

Roosevelt watched Amy and Mrs. Apatosaurus disappear through the trees. Then he heard his mother calling him to dinner. Roosevelt looked around and found that he was not in the forest anymore. He was back in his room. It felt good to be home again. He could smell something good cooking in the kitchen.

Roosevelt thought about his adventure with Amy and her mother, and for the first time he felt like a grown up.

He looked at all the other books he had in his room, and thought of the adventures each one held. Roosevelt smiled and headed to the kitchen for his dinner.

Please send comments and questions to:
Book Buddy Publishing Co., Inc.
16 Lake Oniad Drive
Wappingers Falls, N.Y. 12590

The type is set in Goudy Old Style.
The printing and binding are done by Print Craft, Inc.
The typesetting is done by Michael Miracle.

v